D0185687

KINGFISHER
An imprint of Kingfisher Publications Plc
New Penderel House, 283–288 High Holborn
London WC1V 7HZ
www.kingfisherpub.com

First published in Sweden by Alfabeta Bokförlag
First published in the UK by Kingfisher 2005
1 3 5 7 9 10 8 6 4 2

Text and illustrations copyright © Lars Klinting 1996

The moral right of the authors, editor and illustrators has been asserted.

A CIP catalogue record for this book is available from the British Library.

ISBN-10: 0 7534 1175 X
ISBN-13: 978 0 7534 1175 9

Printed in Taiwan
1TR/0205/SHENS/SGCH/158MA/F

Harvey the Carpenter

Lars Klinting

KINGFISHER

Harvey is planning to make a toolbox today.

All the tools Harvey needs are in his workshop, but it isn't very tidy. Sometimes it's hard for him to find things. Where on earth did he put his plan?

Phew! Here it is. Now he can get started.

First Harvey studies his drawing carefully.
He doesn't want to make any mistakes.

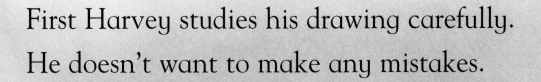

Then Harvey gets his tools ready. He takes out a . . .

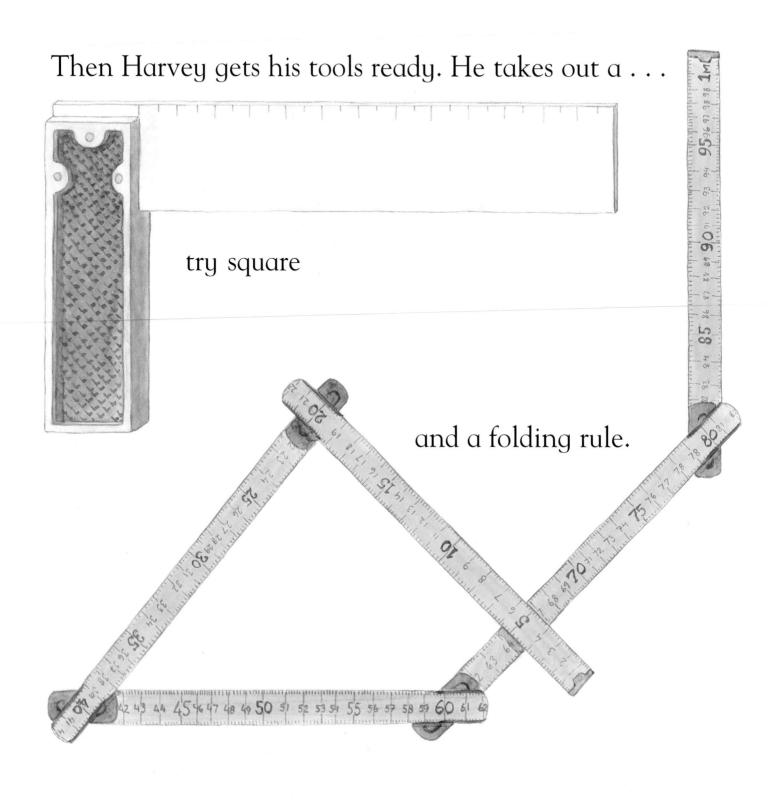

try square

and a folding rule.

Harvey measures the boards
carefully and marks where he is going to cut the
wood. The try square helps him draw straight lines.

Now it's time to use the saw!

Be careful, Harvey –
a saw is very sharp!

Harvey saws the boards along the lines he drew.

He needs a different tool for cutting curved pieces.

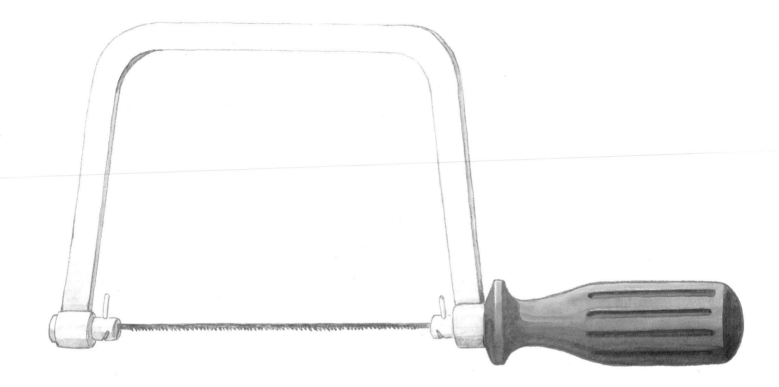

This is a coping saw.

That looks perfect! What a nice,
neat job Harvey has done.

Now Harvey wants
to make some holes.

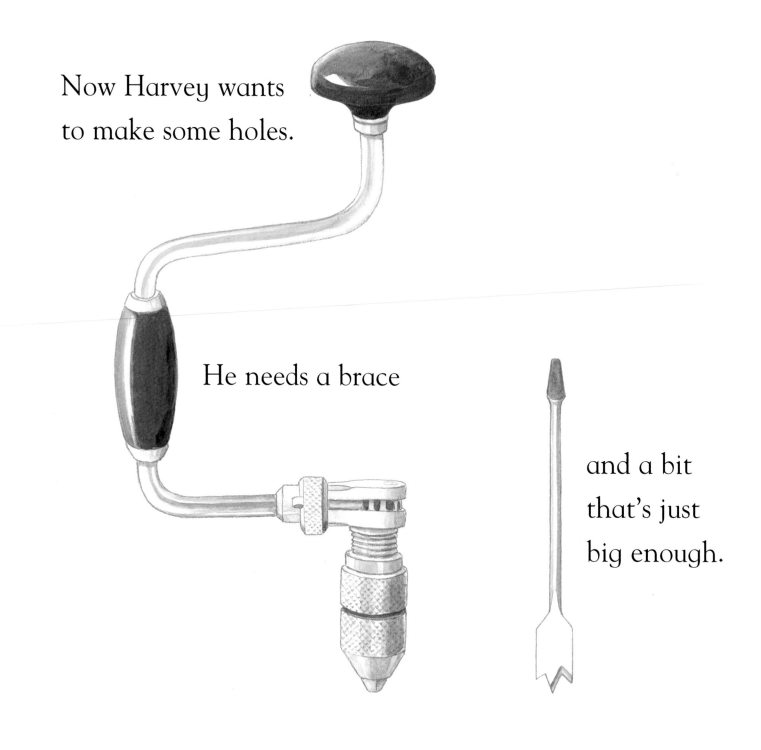

He needs a brace

and a bit
that's just
big enough.

Boring holes is hard work! Harvey stands on his stool so he can reach.

To make some little
holes, Harvey needs
different tools.
He uses . . .

an eggbeater drill

and a bit that's
just small enough.

Harvey whizzes the eggbeater drill round and round.

The wood is rough, and Harvey doesn't want
to get a splinter. He needs to smooth down
the wood with . . .

a rasp file

some sandpaper

and a sanding block.

Harvey rubs the wood for a long time with
the sandpaper. When he's finished,
it feels lovely and smooth!

All the parts are ready, so Harvey
needs to fit them together.

He uses a screwdriver

and some screws.

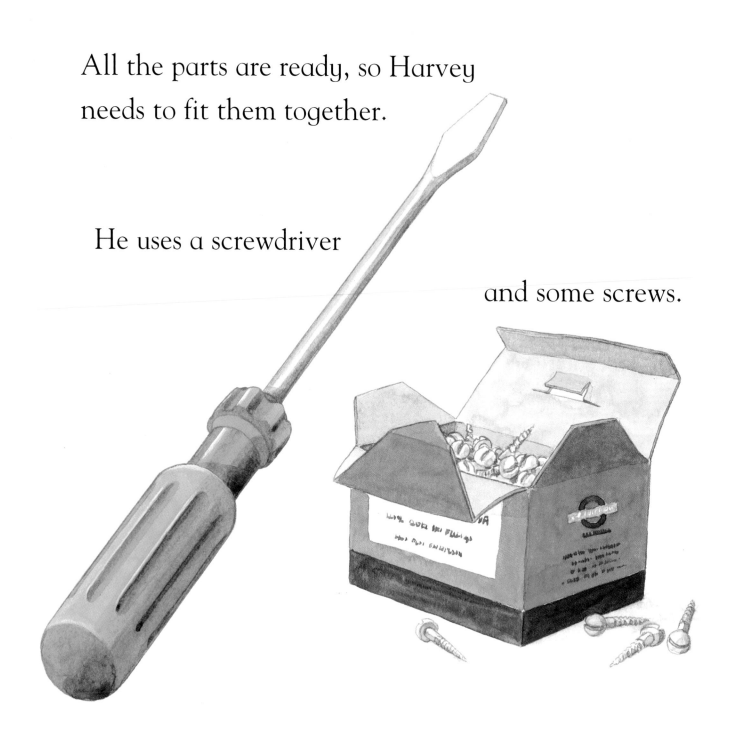

Harvey twists the screws
into the little holes he
made. They fit perfectly!

For the next job, Harvey
needs a hammer . . .

and some nails.

Whoops! Harvey bends one of the nails.

A pair of pliers will sort it out.

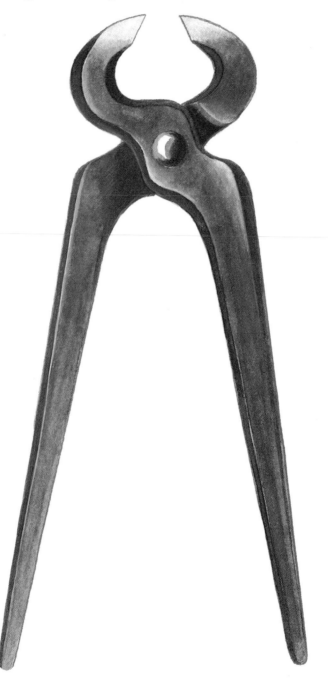

Yank! Harvey tugs out the bent nail. It puts up quite a fight!

The toolbox is almost done.
All Harvey needs
now is . . .

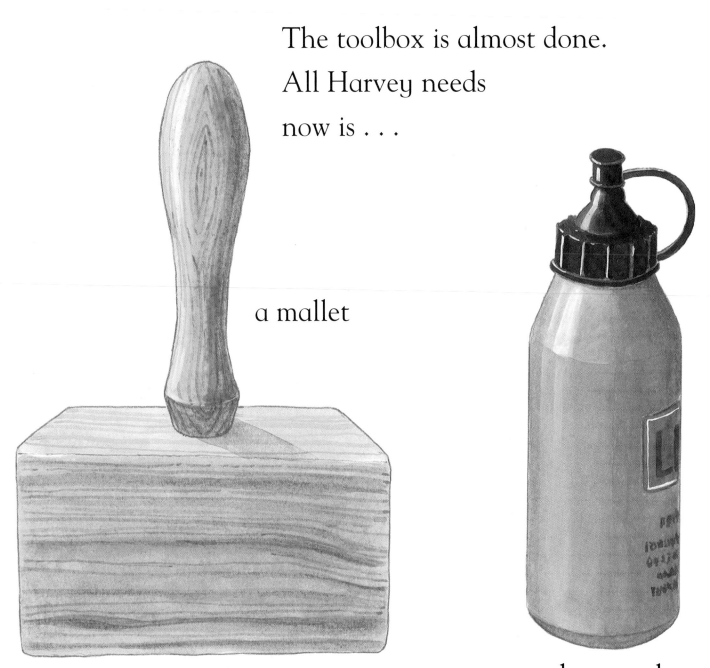

a mallet

and some glue.

Harvey fits the toolbox's handle into the big holes
he bored. A bit of glue will keep it in place.

Now Harvey collects up all his tools. . .

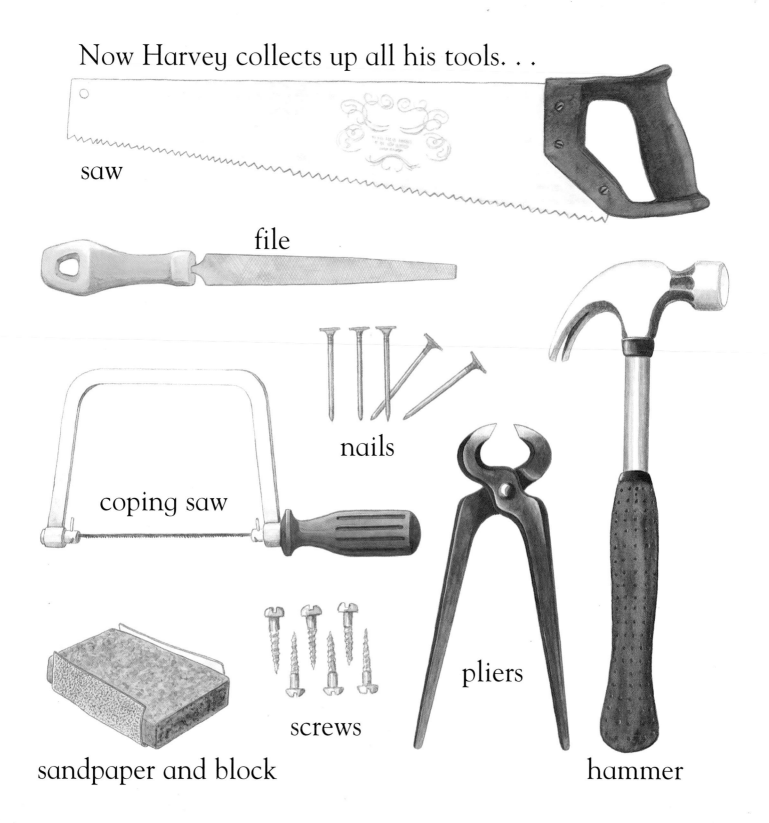

saw

file

nails

coping saw

pliers

hammer

screws

sandpaper and block

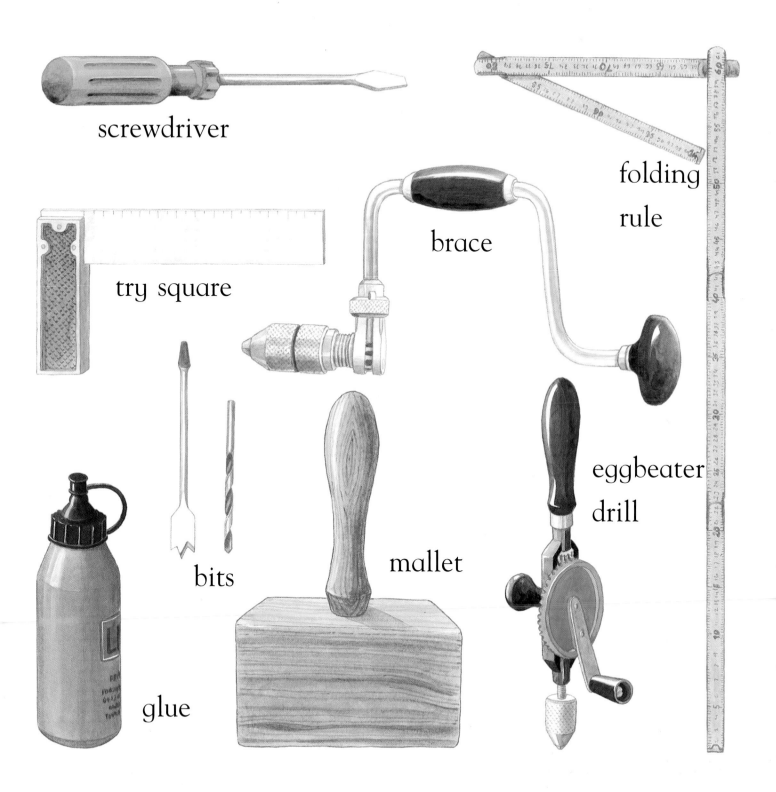

screwdriver

folding rule

try square

brace

bits

mallet

eggbeater drill

glue

. . And puts them away in his brand-new toolbox!

Harvey has worked hard – now it's time for a cup of tea.

Harvey's Toolbox

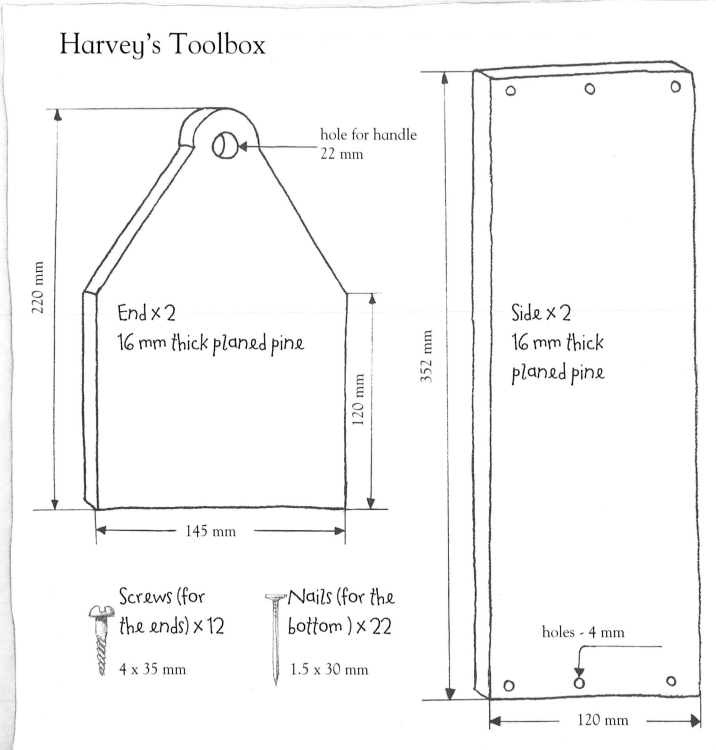

hole for handle
22 mm

220 mm

End × 2
16 mm thick planed pine

120 mm

145 mm

352 mm

Side × 2
16 mm thick
planed pine

Screws (for the ends) × 12

4 × 35 mm

Nails (for the bottom) × 22

1.5 × 30 mm

holes - 4 mm

120 mm

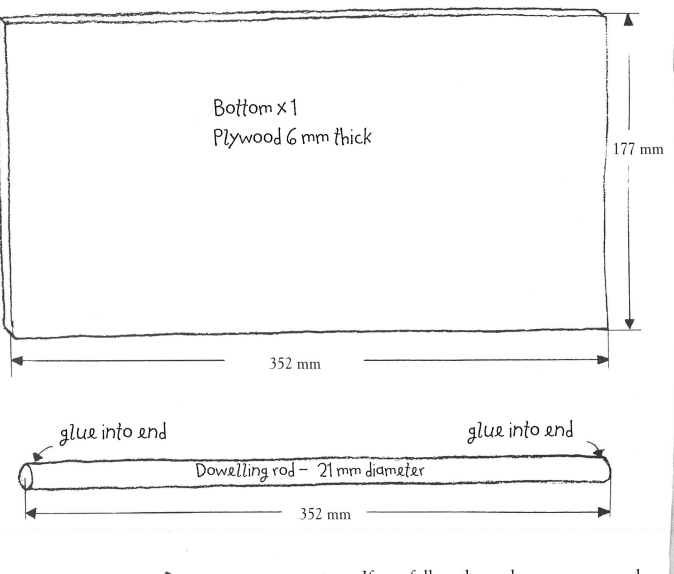

Bottom × 1
Plywood 6 mm thick

177 mm

352 mm

glue into end   glue into end

Dowelling rod – 21 mm diameter

352 mm

If you follow these plans, you can make a toolbox just like Harvey's. But make sure to get an adult to help you!